D0263852

# Contents

# Meet the Mystery Mob

**Name:**

Gummy

**FYI:** Gummy hasn't got much brain – and even fewer teeth.

**Loves:** Soup.

**Hates:** Toffee chews.

**Fact:** The brightest thing about him is his shirt.

**Name:**

Lee

**FYI:** If Lee was any cooler he'd be a cucumber.

**Loves:** Hip-hop.

**Hates:** Hopscotch.

**Fact:** He has his own designer label (which he peeled off a tin).

**Name:**

**FYI:** Rob lives in his own world – he's just visiting planet Earth.

**Loves:** Daydreaming.

**Hates:** Nightmares.

**Fact:** Rob always does his homework – he just forgets to write it down.

**Name:**

Dwayne

**FYI:** Dwayne is smarter than a tree full of owls.

**Loves:** Anything complicated.

**Hates:** Join-the-dots books.

**Fact:** If he was any brighter you could use him as a floodlight at football matches.

**Name:**

Chet

**FYI:** Chet is as brave as a lion with steel jaws.

**Loves:** Having adventures.

**Hates:** Knitting.

**Fact:** He's as tough as the chicken his granny cooks for his tea.

**Name:**

Adi

**FYI:** Adi is as happy as a football fan with tickets to the big match.

**Loves:** Telling jokes.

**Hates:** Moaning minnies.

**Fact:** He knows more jokes than a jumbo joke book.

# Mapping it Out

Dwayne is really excited. He's bought
a dusty old book from a junk shop
and he's found a map hidden inside it!
He can't wait to show the map
to the rest of the Mystery Mob.
They all meet up at Dwayne's house.

**Dwayne**  Look, guys, I've found
this brilliant old map.
It shows the coast near Smugglers'
Cave. And guess what?
Someone's marked an 'X' on it.

**Gummy**    That's bad. You should
take it straight back to the shop.
There's no way I'd buy a map
that someone's already
written on.

**Adi**    Duh. Dwayne's map is
a pirate treasure map
from the olden days.
'X' marks the spot
where the treasure's hidden.

**Gummy**    No way!

**Dwayne**  Well, I'm not sure –
but it could be.

**Lee**  Listen up. Smugglers' Cave
is only a couple of miles away.
We can get there in no time
on our bikes. So why don't we go
and check it out?

**Chet**  Count me in. I'm up
for a pirate treasure hunt.

**Rob**  Hang on a minute.
It's Smugglers' Cave,
so won't it be *smugglers*
who've hidden the loot –
not pirates?

9

**Gummy** Who cares? Treasure is treasure!

**Dwayne** That's right. And when
we find it we'll all be mega rich!

**Rob** *If* we find it.

**Gummy** Of course we'll find it.
We're the Mystery Mob –
and I've got a metal detector.

**Lee** Awesome.

**Rob**      Er … but isn't Smugglers' Cave
supposed to be haunted?

**Dwayne**   Yes, people say it's haunted
by the ghost of a smuggler
called the Ghastly Ghoul.

**Adi**      It's true! Hey, do you know
why ghouls are covered in
wrinkles?

**Rob**      No.

**Adi**      Well, have you ever tried
ironing one?

**Chet**     Grrrr! You'd better hope
we don't meet up
with the Ghastly Ghoul, Adi,
'cos he'll make you
walk the plank of his ghost ship
for telling a joke like that!

# 2

# No Entry

The treasure hunt gets off to a bad start.
Adi and Chet's bikes have flat tyres,
so they can't go. Then a dog runs in front
of Rob's bike. Rob swerves to miss it
and crashes into Lee. They both end up
with buckled bike wheels and have to go
to the bike repair shop. In the end, only
Dwayne and Gummy make it
to the coast.

**Dwayne**  Right. According to my map,
Smugglers' Cave is very near
here.

**Gummy**  Cool. Hey, look, there's a path
going down from the cliff
to the beach. I bet it'll lead us
to the cave.

**Dwayne**  Okay. Let's give it a try.

The boys follow the narrow path.
It ends on the beach right next to a large,
spooky-looking cave.

**Gummy**  Yes! What did I tell you?
This must be Smugglers' Cave.
Right. I'll switch on
the metal detector.

**Dwayne**  Calm down, Gummy.
We've got to wait
until we're inside the cave
before we can start looking
for treasure.

**Gummy**  Good point.

**Dwayne**  Well, I am the one
with the brains.

**Gummy**   Yes, but I'm the one
with the metal detector.

**Dwayne**   Hang on. There's a woman
running along the beach,
and she's waving at us.
I wonder what she wants.

**Gummy**   Search me. Oh, I bet she's
going to tell us it's against the law
to go treasure hunting
in the cave.

The woman comes up to Dwayne and Gummy, and smiles at them.

**Woman**   Hi guys. What are you up to?

**Gummy**   Nothing.

**Woman**   Right. So why are you trying to hide a metal detector behind your back?

**Gummy**   It's not a metal detector – it's an extra long stick of silver rock.

**Woman** Okay, I believe you.
But loads of people
wouldn't.

**Dwayne** Sorry. But we thought
you were going to stop us
from metal detecting
in Smugglers' Cave.

**Woman** Well, I'm sorry to be a pain, guys,
but the cave isn't safe.

**Gummy** Oh right. You mean because
it's haunted by the ghost
of the Ghastly Ghoul?
But don't worry about us.
We're not scared. If we meet him
I'll just hit him with my
metal detector.

**Woman**  I bet you would too.
No, the truth is that the cave
is very dark and full
of jagged rocks. You could trip
and break your legs.
And nobody would ever find you
– except for maybe
the Ghastly Ghoul!

**Gummy**  (gulping) Nasty.

**Woman**  Very. Anyway, look at the sign
over there.

The boys see a sign next to the mouth
of the cave. It says: DANGER! NO ENTRY!
KEEP OUT!

**Dwayne**  Fair enough.
We can't argue with that.

**Gummy**  Oh no, can't we just nip in
and have a quick go?

**Woman**  (sadly) I'm really sorry,
but I don't think so.
I'd never forgive myself
if you guys got hurt.

**Dwayne** Come on, Gummy. She's right.
It's too dangerous.
I guess we'd better go home.

**Woman** Good call, guys.
It's the smart thing to do.

Dwayne and Gummy go back up the path to the top of the cliff.

# ❸

# It's a Fake

**Gummy** I'm totally gutted.
I was looking forward to using
my metal detector. I just know
we would have found
the treasure.

**Dwayne** And we still might.

**Gummy** How?

**Dwayne** We're not giving up.
There's something odd
going on here, and I want
to find out what it is.

**Gummy**   What do you mean?

**Dwayne**   Well, it's just hit me that the
'Danger, No Entry' sign is a fake.

**Gummy**   How come?

**Dwayne**   It didn't have the town council
logo on it. And the sign
was written in felt-tip pen.
Anyone could have put it there.

**Gummy**   But we can't just go in there,
can we? How do we know
it's not really dangerous?

**Dwayne**  Look, my cousin works
at the town hall.
I'll give him a ring
and ask him
to check it out
for us.

Dwayne gets out his mobile and rings
his cousin. It doesn't take long
to get the answer.

**Dwayne**  Result!

**Gummy**  So your cousin says it's okay
to go in the cave?

**Dwayne**  Yes – he says there's no problem
with the cave from the council's
point of view.

**Gummy**  But then who put the sign there –
and why?

**Dwayne**  That's what we're going
to find out. There's something
in that cave that someone
doesn't want us to know about.

**Gummy**  Okay, so what's the plan?

**Dwayne**  We'll hide our bikes
in the bushes, and then
we'll sneak back down to the cave
and take a look inside.

**Gummy**  But what about that nice lady?
I don't want to upset her.

**Dwayne**  Oh, she'll be long gone
by the time we get back
to the cave. Anyway,
it's getting dark, so no one
will spot us.

**Gummy**  Er … let's hope that goes
for the Ghastly Ghoul as well.

**Dwayne**  Oh, I *really* wish you hadn't
said that!

The boys creep back down the path
to Smugglers' Cave.

# Into the Dark

Dwayne and Gummy tiptoe past the
KEEP OUT sign. They go into the dark
cave. It's very cold and spooky. It feels
like they are heading into deadly danger.

**Gummy**    Hurry up and turn on the torch,
Dwayne. I can't see a thing.

**Dwayne**    Okay. Now, switch on
the metal detector
and let's see what we can find.

Gummy waves the detector around, but nothing happens.

**Gummy** It's no good. It's not making a single beep. We'll have to go deeper into the cave.

**Dwayne** Great. There's nothing I love more than creeping around in a dark cave.

**Gummy** And don't forget it's haunted.

**Dwayne** Gummy.

**Gummy** What is it?

**Dwayne** Please <u>shut up</u>.

**Gummy** Right.

The boys go further into the cave.
Their feet slip on the wet stones.
Shadows jump across the rock walls.
It's horrible. They're both scared stiff.

**Dwayne**  I don't like it in here.

**Gummy**  Me neither.

**Dwayne**  Let's pack it in and come back
with the others tomorrow,
when it's light.

**Gummy**  That works for me.

Suddenly, the metal detector
starts to bleep.

**Gummy**  Hey, we've found something!

**Dwayne**  All right! Let's dig.

The boys soon dig up a wooden box.
They open it. It's full of watches, money,
gold rings and jewels.

**Gummy**   Wow – it *is* treasure.

**Dwayne**   Yeah, but it's not old stuff.
Pirates and smugglers
didn't bury this. My guess is
we've found a modern burglar's
secret stash.

**Gummy**   Oh. Hey, what was that?

From somewhere in the darkness,
the boys hear the sound of footsteps
coming towards them.

# ⑤

# The Ghastly Ghoul

**Gummy**   Quick – turn off the torch!

**Dwayne**   Too late!

Dwayne's torch shines on the scary face
of the Ghastly Ghoul! The Ghastly Ghoul
cackles. And comes closer.

**Gummy**   What are we going to do,
Dwayne?

**Dwayne**   I dunno.

**Gummy**   Well, hurry up
and think of something.
This is really stressing me out!

Dwayne and Gummy back away. Then
they bump into solid rock. They're at the
end of the cave. They are trapped!

**Gummy**   We're soooo dead.

**Dwayne**   Shut up, Gummy.

But the Ghastly Ghoul stops. It grabs
the box and dashes off into the darkness.

**Dwayne**   Hey, that's not the Ghastly
Ghoul. That must be the burglar.

**Gummy**   Come on, he's getting away
with the loot.

The boys give chase.

**Dwayne**  It's no good.
He's too quick for us.

**Gummy**  Wait a sec. I've got an idea.

Gummy takes aim with his metal detector.
He throws it at the burglar.
It hits the burglar's legs. He trips up
and falls. Gummy and Dwayne
jump on his back.

**Dwayne** Quick. Tie his hands
and feet together with your belt.

**Gummy** Okay, but don't blame me
if my trousers fall down.

**Dwayne** Hmmmm …
the burglar's wearing
a Ghastly Ghoul face mask.
Let's take it off and see
who he really is.

Dwayne pulls off the mask.
The boys get a big surprise.

**Gummy**  I don't believe it!
It's the nice lady from the beach!

**Dwayne**  Yes, only she's not so nice
after all.

**Gummy**  You're not kidding.
Come on, lady, who are you?

**Woman**  Grrrr … I'm Lucy Lastic,
the world's best burglar.
I rob from posh houses
and hide the loot in this cave.
No one ever comes here –
they're too scared they'll meet
the Ghastly Ghoul.

**Dwayne**  But you put that KEEP OUT sign
outside the cave just to make sure,
didn't you?

**Woman** That's right. And everything was going fine until you two pesky kids came along.

**Dwayne** Yeah, but you never stood a chance against us.

**Woman** Why not?

**Gummy** Well, we are just way too cool for ghouls!

# About the author

Roger Hurn has:

- been an actor in 'The Exploding Trouser Company'
- played bass guitar in a rock band
- been given the title Malam Oga (wise teacher, big boss!) while on a storytelling trip to Africa.

Now he's a writer, and he hopes you like reading about the Mystery Mob as much as he likes writing about them.

# The pirate quiz

**Questions**

1 What does a pirate Santa Claus say?

2 How much did the pirate pay for his peg leg and hook?

3 Why do pirates always carry a bar of soap?

4 What do you get when you cross a rat and a pie?

5 Why did the pirate's phone go beep, beep, beep?

6 Where can you find a pirate who's lost both his peg legs?

7 What would you do if you saw a fierce pirate armed with a cutlass coming towards you?

8 Where do pirate ships go when they're ill?

Answers

1 Yo Ho Ho.

2 An arm and a leg.

3 So, if they are shipwrecked, they can wash themselves ashore!

4 A pie rat (pirate – get it?!)

5 Because he left it off the hook!

6 In the same place you left him.

7 Hope he was going to a fancy-dress party.

8 To the dock.

## How did you score?

👋 If you got all eight pirate answers correct, then you are the captain of the ship!

👋 If you got six pirate answers correct, then you're ready to be the first mate.

👋 If you got fewer than four pirate answers correct, then it's time for you to walk the plank!

# When I was a kid

**Question**  Did you go looking for buried treasure when you were a kid?

**Roger**  Yes. My dad said our house once belonged to a pirate. He told me that the pirate had buried his treasure chest in the back garden, but nobody had ever found it.

**Question**  So what did you do?

**Roger**  I got my dad's spade and dug up the whole back garden.

**Question**  Did you find the pirate's treasure chest?

**Roger**  No, my dad was fibbing. There wasn't one.

**Question**  So why did he tell you there was?

**Roger**  The back garden needed weeding and he was too lazy to do it.

# Adi's favourite pirate joke

Do you know how a pirate ship cuts through the waves?

It uses a sea-saw!

# How to hunt for treasure

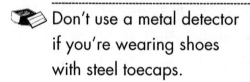

Always get permission
before you go digging holes –
otherwise you could find *yourself* in a hole.

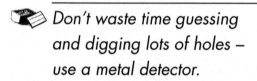

*Don't waste time guessing
and digging lots of holes –
use a metal detector.*

Don't use a metal detector
if you're wearing shoes
with steel toecaps.

*Don't dig a hole on a crowded beach*
*and shout, 'Treasure!' —*
*unless you want to be*
*trampled to death in the rush.*

If you do find any gold or silver,
don't rush off and spend it.
All gold and silver treasure
belongs to the Queen. Doh!
Life can be so unfair!

# Fantastic facts about pirates

**1**   No one has ever found a real pirate treasure map. The bad news is that they only exist in stories!

**2**   Pirates wore gold and silver earrings because they believed they improved their eyesight. So that's why you've never seen a pirate wearing glasses!

**3**   Pirates wore eye patches because a patch was cheaper and more comfy than a glass eye. A patch also kept muck out of the empty eye hole!

**4**   No pirates had hooks for hands. They needed both hands to be able to sail the pirate ship. News Flash! Captain Hook is a character in a book – he isn't real.

**5**   Unlike Long John Silver, real pirates who lost a leg didn't replace them with wooden ones. They used crutches.

# Pirate lingo

**Black spot**  A pirate with a 'Black spot' doesn't have a big boil on his face. It means other pirates want to kill him.

**Davy Jones' locker**  The bottom of the sea.

**Jolly Roger**  The pirates' skull-and-crossbones flag – not the writer of this book when he's in a good mood.

**Shiver me timbers**  Pirates said this when they were really surprised. It sounds better than saying, "No way!"

**Walk the plank**  The pirates' way of getting rid of prisoners. Actually, this only happens in pirate movies. Real pirates just threw their prisoners overboard. Nice!

# Mystery Mob

## Mystery Mob Set 1:

Mystery Mob and the Abominable Snowman
Mystery Mob and the Big Match
Mystery Mob and the Circus of Doom
Mystery Mob and the Creepy Castle
Mystery Mob and the Haunted Attic
Mystery Mob and the Hidden Treasure
Mystery Mob and the Magic Bottle
Mystery Mob and the Missing Millions
Mystery Mob and the Monster on the Moor
Mystery Mob and the Mummy's Curse
Mystery Mob and the Time Machine
Mystery Mob and the UFO

## Mystery Mob Set 2:

Mystery Mob and the Ghost Town
Mystery Mob and the Bonfire Night Plot
Mystery Mob and the April Fools' Day Joker
Mystery Mob and the Great Pancake Day Race
Mystery Mob and the Scary Santa
Mystery Mob and the Conker Conspiracy
Mystery Mob and the Top Talent Contest
Mystery Mob and the Night in the Waxworks
Mystery Mob and the Runaway Train
Mystery Mob and the Wrong Robot
Mystery Mob and the Day of the Dinosaurs
Mystery Mob and the Man-eating Tiger

# RISING ★ STARS

**Mystery Mob books are available from most booksellers.**

**For mail order information
please call Rising Stars on Freephone 0800 091 1602
or visit www.risingstars-uk.com**